First published in Australia by HiveMind Press 2022.

Copyright © HiveMind Press, 2022.

ISBN: 978-0-6454821-2-6

Typeset/Cover Design by - HiveMind Press

Artwork by: Jessica Sierra.

ELEMENTAL ECHOES

ECHOES

Tales of Earth's Enchantment

I wrote this for you,
and for the Earth
we all call home.

Contents

The
Deepest
Caress

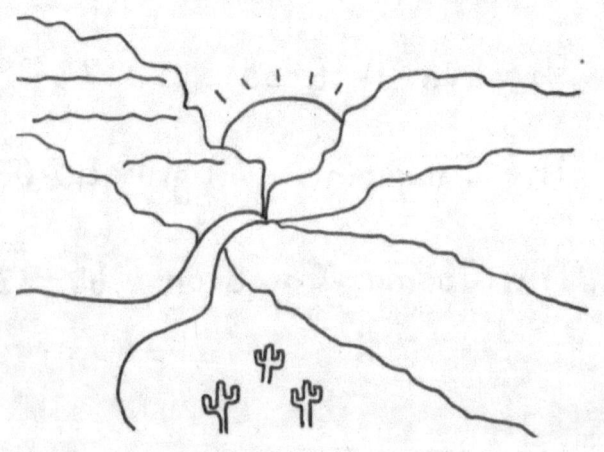

1

Once upon a time,
about five or six million
years ago, the world's
greatest love story began.
Before the magnitude
and magnificence of the
Grand Canyon became
visible to human eyes,
the Colorado River fell
in love with the rich,
red rock. Long before we
began to awe at sunsets
melting
into
striking strata

-as vistas s t r e t c h
beyond our line of vision-
the river had a vision of
what was to come. * * * *
Meandering along the
canyon floor, cutting and
carving channels through
chromatic crust, she never
lost focus of her dream.

Carefully caressing the
land that she loved, she
s t r e t c h e d her
entire body across him.
The Earth was firm

and fixed in his ways,
stubborn to her loving
touch. She did not falter.
She knew the beauty that
lay beneath his skin, long
before we could see. As
she persisted with her
gentle, undulating flow,
the Earth softened. He
allowed her to undress
him. Soil and sediment
safe in her embrace, she
carried him across the
continent. Giving her
solid ground beneath the

myriad of tributaries she
e x t e n d e d over his
limbs, he held her, and
constellations formed
explanations for the
exploration that their
bodies embarked.

Two elements, meeting and
merging, passionately
intertwining. Sensually and
s l o w l y, just as she had
known all along, the Earth
opened, revealing his warm
inside and exquisite layers

of vividly coloured rock.
   Layer
               upon
                      layer
of ancient history held
within his body, he was
venerable with his
vulnerability to expose
his insides for all of
the world to see.

Each stratum is a
different colour that
represents a different era
of time - reds, ochres,
yellows, buffs - intricate
lines seemingly painted

onto the walls that he
let crumble. For her, and
her love. Her soft, soothing
strokes continue to deepen
and w i d e n the canyon
today, as the grandeur
of their love is put into
perspective for all the
world
to
see.

The Lair
of Lava

Once upon a time, only about one or two million years ago, when Earth existed in her feminine form, dragons nestled in the picturesque troglodyte village we now know as Göreme in central Turkey. It was a time after the noble dragons left, departing this world for another. The hearth in their hearts was no longer fuelled with excitement or rich creative spark. It was rage. It

was greed. The colossal
creatures were restless.
They were reckless. Their
wisdom was deep, but
their gluttony was toxic.
Despite their capacity to
zoom in on prey far away,
they could not foresee their
own wrath. Hungering for
the jewels nestled within
Earth's skin, they clawed
into her crust with their
sharp, razorblade talons. An
innate and all-encompassing
peace emanated from Earth's

core, enriching her with patience, empathy and understanding. In a low tone with slow articulation, she warned the dragons to stop.

"You must look within yourselves to find gold. Not pillage the planet."

The dragons knew better. They chose not to change. Quenching a thirst that they could not satisfy;

they always wanted more.
They continued thrusting
their tails into Earth's
crust, selfishness hardening
their once-soft skin. As
they cracked Earth open,
a deep, stabbing pain
oscillated into her core.
Through steaming chambers,
her mantle and crust

connected in volcanos
mounding from the lacerations.
Her skin was broken like a
sundered shield, revealing
her sheltered heart to the
vulnerability of her rupture
that was her rapture. For
being broken is how we
open. We must destroy the
old before we can create
something new. Shooting hot
magma from three volcanoes
formed from the dragons'
claws, she watched it
stream into the dragons'

nest. The gases she excreted
were poisonous to the beasts,
for her love-filled breath
was a medicine the dragons
did not know how to swallow.
Slowly but surely, the dragons
withered and waned, destroyed
by their own vile greed.
The dragons couldn't change
their ways fast enough to
save themselves. But
maybe us humans can.

When the ash settled,
and their era evanesced,

Earth was fragile. The entire Cappadocian plateau was strewn with destruction. Volcanic ash consolidated, creating light porous rock, and from the rubble, the rebuilding began. The Earth continues to change face, transforming through time. She promised she would never crack open her heart in that part again. In reverence for the mighty beasts, though they lost their way, she plateaued part of herself where the dragons' lair once lay.

In the years that followed, she allowed herself to cry. To heal by letting herself feel. To find peace through release. Sometimes her tears cascaded from the sky in torrential rainstorms that drowned out her rational mind and eroded soft layers of lava and ash into spindly stems of surreal enchantment. Other times,

she iced over, becoming
cynical to love and life
in despair of the destruction.
Eventually she found hope.
Her demeanour warmed
with the golden nectar of
dripping sunshine
that melted
away her melancholy as
she embraced the future's
mystery with optimism and
pride. It was her swift
climatic change-her courage
to embrace all facets of
her abundant emotions-that

transformed the ruin
into the riveting rocks
we see today.

It was the captivating
caverns carved from wind
and water washing away
the warfare that compelled
the fairies to come. When
they arrived thousands of
years ago, they built chimneys
from their underground homes
in tall, thin rock spires
protruding out from the
arid Anatolian Earth.

They fluttered with joy
and flattered Earth for
her beauty. Her inherent
power. Her unwavering poise.
Her inspiring perseverance.

Filling the sky with song,
the vivacious creatures
sent healing vibrations
deep into Earth's core.
The Earth resonates with
the pure of heart and
sprouted wildflowers for
the fairies to tie around
their naked bodies.

Delighting in the floral fragrances, they played chasey in the sky. "Tag, you're it!" they cheered, coating Earth's contours with honeycomb and cream fairy dust. Different eras of Earth's emotion streaked the strata. Yellow tips show the fairies' joy. Layers of pink and red, the bleeding of her heart, stratified over the white and grey wisdom and purity she gained from her pain.

Eventually, as with all
inhabitants of Earth, the
time came for the fairies
to go. Transcending the
lunarscape they loved so
dearly, the fairies relocated
to the moon. From there,
they admire Earth with
tender love.
Sometimes
you can glimpse
them fluttering
across the
night sky in a
glistening stream

of light. Their airborne
magic often appears as
shimmering shooting stars.
Look a little
closer.
Listen
a little
deeper.

Can you hear the
fairies singing for us
to treat our Earth with
the reverence that
she deserves?

The Era
of Eros

South America and
Antarctica reach for
each other like star-
crossed lovers, separated
by the furious waves
and howling winds of
three oceans converging.
In the world's largest
and roughest current,
1000 kilometres of wild
undercurrents crash in
a clockwise motion.
About three hundred
million years ago, when
Antarctica was warmer

than California and
covered in lush evergreen
forests, the world existed
as one massive super
continent, Pangea.

In this Permian period
of unity, South America
and Antarctica fell
                        in
                          love.

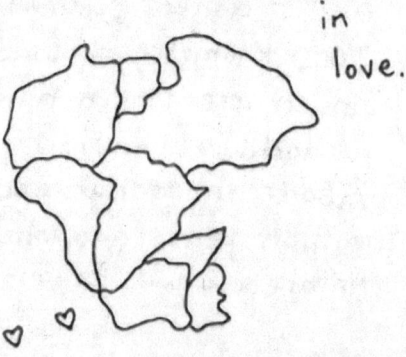

It was an impassioned affair. An era of eros. A soft and slow journey, enriched with the tender nectar of deep devotion. The Ice Queen adored the quiet warmth of South America's ardent touch. Her Latino Lover cherished the unwavering safety that glistened through her cool, calm nature.

As earthquakes, volcanic eruptions and subterranean

movements caused the supercontinent to stretch, thin and f-fragment about 180 million years ago, the lovers were p u l l e d apart. Their parting was painful. Physically they could not touch. Emotionally, their bond remained in oceanic tides that kept them connected. The other continents supported the separated lovers through their heartache. They literally

had their backs. Africa
spooned South America
in a platonic embrace.
Similarly, India and
Australasia held Antarctica's
north-western shores with
caring hands. Eventually,
as time ticked on and
rifting continued to
split the continents apart,
Africa, India and
Australasia respectively
broke away, bound for
other horizons.

With no friends to
mitigate their pain,
the Ice Queen and
her Latino Lover had
the space to focus on
the purity of their love
with clarity and appreciation.
As affection rippled into
their deepest tectonic
layers, the Earth's
lithosphere shifted and
lifted again, responding
to the lovers' longing
to reconnect. In the
Cretaceous period, 65

million years ago, the
Ice Queen and her
Latino Lover touched
once more. Electricity
cascaded through plains
and valleys, as rivers
and ridges bridged
their eternal bond. In
a silky rhythm, their
bodies moved, rising
and falling like ocean
waves. Destined to meet.
Destined to retreat.
Destined to repeat the
cycle. Their last goodbye

staggered over hundreds of thousands of years as plate tectonics p u l l e d them apart once more. When the Drake Passage opened about 41 million years ago, the inception of the world's largest ocean current - the Antarctica Circumpolar - was felt worldwide.

Today, South America and Antarctica extend

themselves into the
wild waters that
simultaneously separate
and connect. With no
resistance from nearby
landmasses, the tempestuous
ocean passage is a
pummelling no-man's-land
defined by two moods:
the "Drake Lake", when
still and serene
the continents
share a restful reverie,
or the "Drake Shake",
when lovesickness brings

chaotic storms that churn
like a washing
machine with
hurricane force.
From beaches they reach,
but they can never quite
meet. Pondering the
could haves, would haves,
should haves- is it better
to feel true love and lose
it, or never touch it at all?

There was a time when
the ocean's intensity
reflected the lovers'

internal world. Guarded
and suspicious, they were
fearful of loving again.
He burned with agony.
She froze to bitter ice.
Their once connected
shores sharpened to
ragged headlands that
notoriously swallowed
seafarers in a deathly
abyss. The Latino Lover
dreamed of the Ice
Queen's devoted arms
enriched by steep, snowy,
sparkly peaks. It was

harrowing and confusing to taste true love and lose it. But it hurts more to never touch it at all. The Ice Queen yearned for the striking black cliffs of Cape Horn, her beloved's southern tip. There, he barricaded his heart with rocky ramparts in cynical hope it would prohibit him from ever being hurt again. He soon learned it wouldn't stop him from hurting. It stopped him from loving and blocked him from being loved. And that hurt more.

Over time, the solitude of the sea was cleansing. The lovers discerned that life is comprised of both pleasure and pain. Love hurts. But it heals too. Over time, the wild and untamed Pacific merged with the dense, salty Atlantic. Together, they soothed heartache's jagged edges and smoothed the lovers' pain with tender memories of treasured days. Over time, rough rocks became polished pebbles that people skimmed across the water as ripples creased still surfaces with the potency of interconnectedness and impact.

To love and be loved is the greatest feeling on Earth. It comes with corresponding fears and responsibilities, but genuine love cannot be lost. For it is born in the part of us that does not die. Even as tectonic plates continue to manoeuvre the world into new positions, their love forever remains. Spiralling upwards in a unified bliss towards heaven and extending down to the passionate mantle, South America and Antarctica will continue to outstretch their arms — cherishing their memories, holding sacred

the pleasure and growth
they shared, keeping their
communication channels
open through the emotion
of the ocean in constant
motion.

The
Tangerine
Twilight

Long ago, before we
created navigational
compasses enabling us to
chart our location in the
open ocean and thus map
the world, an innate wisdom
was known and revered
by our ancestral tribes.

It was that of the
elements - Earth, Fire,
Water, Air - the four
fundamental forces that
create our fabric of life. In
a time when our family

tree was much smaller, our
ancient forefathers gathered
every dusk and dawn.
Sunny, snowy, stormy or
still, they sang into the
tangerine twilight:
  "Earth my body
  Water my blood
  Air my breath and
  Fire my spirit."

Each element is composed
of deep-rooted shadows
and gifts. Strong and
stable, Earth took steady

strides to build substance over long periods of time. She taught the others patience and allowed them to ground into her solid being, giving nourishment to grow. By nature, she could root so firmly into dried-up beliefs, she became crusted in a dry trench and was unyielding to change.

With a dash of daring, Fire inspired her to open with his illuminating spark. His

warmth was invigorating,
stirring high ideals with an
infectious zest for life.
Fire was bold and
bewitching. The speed
with which he ignited with
tremendous passion was
thrilling, unless his fuel
was rage.

Water's calming currents
cooled Fire's heat when
needed. Fluid and flowing,
completely drenched in
feeling, her psychic depths

were a blessing and a curse. Her acute sensitivity enabled compassion and care that cleansed away impurity, allowing an osmosis of intuition and imagination to flow. Sometimes, though, she swam too deep, drowning in a desire to escape it all.

That's when Air breezed in, with a curiosity and charm lightening the load. He transcended the murky

world of feelings to the
clear mental stratosphere,
where fresh ideas and
information glided into his
invisible skin. Omnipresent
and oxygenating, Air was
empowered by Air's ability
to bridge his ideas into reality.

Every month, the elements
convened to commemorate
life. Beneath the inky
black sky of each dark
moon, they met on a
beautiful island in the

Aegean Sea. Earth gifted
Fire broken branches to
fuel his golden glow. Unto
the flames, Air exhaled the
mysterious mist gathered
in his lofty trail. Water
warmed her salty seas,
giving rejuvenation and
replenishment for her
elemental kin.

One cloudy evening, a
sudden vision ignited in
Fire's flames. In a ravenous
frenzy, orange flickers

twisted and curled into
obscure shapes, hypnotising
the elements like a plasma
TV. Burning branches
became an image of human
hands relentlessly slicing
old-growth forests with no
reverence for the ancient
wisdom in each splinter of
every tree. Man
strung massive
wooden trunks
together and
constructed
ships to

conquer the world. Images
of death and destruction
entailed. They massacred
indigenous tribes. Poisonous
gases gushed into the air.
The oceans filled with
toxic pollutants. All in
the name of evolution.

The vision extinguished,
leaving golden embers in
its wake, and a wave of
unease crashed the party.
Air gasped for breath,
gagging for a long, deep

inhale, as though the
irritated tingle of carbon
monoxide was already
seeping into his skin.
Earth ruptured into a fit
of thick, phlegmy coughs
as though trying to rid
the infections that land
degradation would bring.
A single, silent tear fell
from Water's eye in a
salty trickle that rippled
into her entire being.
Fire flared into a wild
inferno, outraged by

the vision that had flashed
to life in <u>his</u> flames.

With a scorching heat,
he roared, "We must burn
them! We must destroy
all humans, before they
destroy us."

Air breezed backwards,
detaching from the
emotional charge with an
aloof air that refused to
fan Fire's flames. The
conversation made him

anxious, as information sped through his nervous system like a falcon diving towards prey.

Water remained silent. On the surface, she was calm. But beneath her composed exterior, she plunged to benthic depths. Fire's words echoed into her psychic realms as she searched for deeper meaning.

It was Earth that broke the

silence, concluding, in a firm, dry tone, "No. I gave an oath to provide for all beings who call me home."

Fire sizzled, "You saw the vision in the flames. These monsters don't deserve you. It will be the beginning of the end."

Earth pondered Fire's raging plan with an admirable practicality, stoic in her emotions. Enduring a self-

control that was stubborn
when necessary, Earth
breathed into her core
and responded, "No.
My word is my word."

Before Fire could fume
back in a vindictive spark,
Air gusted in, "I understand
your anger, Fire. But
destroying humans will
go against our elemental
vows. Lets send a message
instead. A warning of
the devastation that will

come if they lose their
humanity to greed. I will
send messages in the
whispers of the wind, as
I scatter pollen and seeds..."

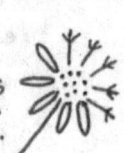

A ruminating silence followed.

Finally, Water gushed in.
"Yes, it's the only way.
The vision was real. It
is inevitable for the world
to be connected. Yes,
there will be death and
destruction. But there is

more. When humanity remembers how it feels to love each other, there will be unity on Earth."

The primal impulse of Fire did not rule Water. Her intuition guided her, flowing into every crack and crevice, then becoming one with her container. When Water spoke, Fire listened. For the ancient elemental codes enabled her to cool his heat and extinguish him, if necessary.

"A message with magnitude is vital," Air breathed. "It will require a sacrifice from us all. For the world to hear us, we must each give a part of ourselves to birth something better."

The elements stayed up all night, solidifying their plan until twilight. Together they fused Air's ideas, Fire's passion, Earth's ambition, and Water's

depth of understanding.
Then the sounds of singing
filled the morning air,
and they embraced in a
bittersweet goodbye.

In the time that followed,
Fire and Earth joined
forces to create magma-
hot molten rock-that Water
deliberately embraced.
Magma's heat turned Water
to steam, creating a volatile
pressure with transferring
thermal energy. As steam

expanded explosively.
Magma tore apart
in a monumental
volcanic eruption.
Rip. Rumble. Roar.
The eruption was equivalent
to the detonation of
forty atomic bombs.

Thick rivers of lava
became blood baths for
the island's original
inhabitants. Water crashed
in massive tsunamis. Every
half hour, titanic waves

struck the
shores of Crete
and crashed
ships into mountains.

Air bore the burden of ash
and dust, along with the
roaring acoustics that were
heard in what is now
modern-day Delhi. After
two days, magma chambers
completely emptied, causing
the volcano to implode.
This thus created the
glimmering caldera of

water connecting what we
now call Santorini. Grey
pumice coated the ocean.
Volcanic ash pierced the
stratosphere, starving Earth
of sunlight and clean air.
It was a cataclysm
bringing a global winter
for two years. Temperatures
dropped, the sun set in
strange colours, and famine
broke out in what is now
modern-day China.

Then there was silence.

Eventually, white Cycladic houses sprinkled over the cresent-shaped island, and the world came to see. Every year, two million tourists awe at tangerine sunsets melting into sapphire seas while snapping postcard-perfect selfies. Santorini is more than just a stunning metaphor of the beauty created from utter destruction. It's more than just a tourist hotspot that enchants us with iconic images

of whitewashed villages
clinging to photogenic cliffs.
Direct from elements that
knit the tapestry of our
lives, it's a message. A
reminder to love each
other, open our hearts and
feel the world's collective
beat. To love our Earth
and live with reverance for
the Mother who homes us.

The
Cosmic
Cauldron

Some time ago-long for
some, recently for others-
a little spark flashed to life
in our parents' eyes. It was
the beginning of our life
on Earth, this tiny twinkle
in the gaze shared between
two lovers. While nebulas
nurture the potential for
new constellations, the same
elements composed in the
hearts of shooting stars
form intricate art in the
meeting and merging of
our parent's genetic codes.

Carbon in our muscles,
oxygen in our lungs,
calcium in our bones,
nitrogen in our DNA, iron
in our blood and hydrogen
forming water in our cells
intertwine into a mass of
flesh and bones that
become the tapestry of
our existence. While DNA
spirals with the foundations
for the journey to unravel,
different constitutions of
earth, air, fire and water
construct and contour the

fabric of us. Swathed in sensation, Earth grounds us in concrete consistency and resourceful rationality. Impassioned by intuition, Fire compels an ignition of enterprising enthusiasm and coruscating courage. Fluid with feeling, Water bathes us in dreamy devotion and tender trust. With tonic thought, Air wraps us in witty wisdom and inquisitive inspiration. In a cosmic cauldron,

our complex layers begin
with a single cell.

The magic of pregnancy
begins before conception,
on the first day of our
mother's last menstrual
cycle. As the outer lining
of her endometrium
sheds, she releases
an old cycle,
making space
for the new.
The body is
wise. It holds

innate, starry wisdom. It knows that the tangibility of new life is inevitable in shedding one's skin. Blood represents death and pain. But it also symbolises the essence of our life force; the inherited genetic codes and personality traits configured from unique elemental intertwining as stardust shimmers and shimmies through our veins. Like the fluid and flowing nature of water moving stagnated emotions in cleansing waves to reveal our deeper layers, there is power in letting the facade fall and allowing ourselves to be seen. Beneath our rigid, rocky exterior is striking strata of intricate emotion – passion like red ribbons of fiery flames, hope like the mellow yellow of flowery fields, despair like the grim grey of haunted hollows and optimism like the tangerine

twilight of a
new day. The same
celestial phenomenon
binds vulnerability and
venerability. For death
and breath are connected
– they link life.

While divinity dances in a
cosmic sea, an amazing
hormonal rhythm enriches
our fluid-filled womb with
darkness. Unconditional love
enriches the space between
mother and child. It is

versatile and viable, yet intimate and innate. As the umbilical cord nurtures and nourishes us with somatic elements that are essential for earthbound life, a stream of light from the centre of our galaxy ripples through our starry-eyed parents and threads the fabric of our being. We are a vessel crossing a vast ocean passage.

completely immersed by water before being birthed into a strange new world. This naval string may be cut, separating us like monumental tectonic movement that creates continental shifts, but our connection will always remain. There will always be a part of mother and child reaching across the starry ocean that connects tombs and wombs.

Written in the stars, or
maybe our genetic code, is
the inevitable pain that
earthbound life entails.
Whether we transform these
wounds into wisdom is a
daily choice we write.
Swirling supernovas foretell
the scorching scars that
come from the fiery breath
of corrupt dragons clawing
at our skin without consent.
Sexual assault ensures a
destructive fire. It
annihilates our insides and

yet ignites an elemental
strength lying dormant in
our bones. In the ashy
aftermath, we are reborn.
Fiery furnaces pulsate
through our veins like
internal volcanos exploding
with lethal shrapnel of
violated boundaries.
Eventually, we choose the
empowered path of
liberation and kindle a new
fire. In the intermittent,
hot magma shoots upwards
and outwards, plateauing a

part of us and forming
novel features like limbs
and organs growing in
our mothers' belly.

Our galactic heritage
extends to the deepest part
of Earth's core and the
furthest reaches of the
cosmos. Souls are stars
gazing upon us from the
place that we reside between
being earthed and birthed.
We feel resonance with
the night sky because the

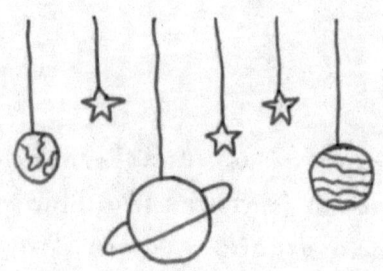

celestial bodies are where
we come from. Twisting
and churning across inky
black skies, stars are
twinkling enchantments of
passion, hope and resolve.
Dark matter brims with
quintessence that sings
for our hearts to beat.
In the third trimester,
the foundations for

consciousness
form with
left and right
hemispherical functioning
occuring in the brain.
Neurones spark like
glittery constellations,
mapping the two greatest
journeys we will ever take:
deep within and far beyond.

When the time comes for
us to enter this life, the
fluid sac containing us
breaks open in preparation.

Moments extend into infinity as powerful contractions pull us through the birthing portal and our mothers push through intense pain. We stretch her flesh as our heads crown. She screams and heaves as tears stream and eventually the agony weaves into ecstasy as she holds us in her loving hands and nebulas explode in her wide eyes. The first breath is a shock to our system. We are waking up

from one dream and entering
the next. Emerging from
the darkness, we are
birthed into the light.

The beginning of our
earthbound life involves
the most pleasurable and
painful experience of life.
Each lap around the
yellow dwarf promises
astronomical fluctuations
between the tests that trial
our quest for smiles and
rifts and blows containing

gifts for us to grow. Sometimes a dense depression sticks to us and clogs these voyages as we trudge forward. Sometimes our thoughts crash against our skull like angry tides or twist and contort like wild tornados replicating DNA spirals that pulsate stardust through our veins. In the storm's eye is a stellar stillness that is the potion

for peace. There is a
time to seed wisdom,
feed happiness, bleed
what must be released
and breed the courage
to rise again. Can you
feel it on the wind as
it shapeshifts
and sings?

Upon fragments
of space rock
shooting across the
Milky Way in combusting
streams of light, my wish

is that you remember
the intrinsic rapture
in your heart's every
beat

that you
leave people and places
better than you found
them, and you experience
the magic of
unconditional love.

Next:

The Unravelling Journey

The Unravelling Journey is a compelling and courageous memoir that spans seven continents, following a young woman transcending the trauma of sexual abuse that sparked a seven-year depression. Think *Eat, Pray, Love* meets *Thirteen Reasons Why* with a dose of *The Alchemist* thrown in for good measure.